<u>Billy</u>

A story by Joe Etheridge

Chapter one: The Cooper's.

It was a cold day, the coldest it had been all year, there were thick grey clouds covering the sky while light rain fell silently to the frost coated ground. The street, Wesley Road, was empty except for a few stray cats searching for shelter from the rain beneath cars and porches. Tall trees that decorated the dull, depressing street swayed back and forth as the chilling wind blew them. The houses were all perfectly set in rows with their perfectly painted walls and perfect gardens. At the end of the street was a house that stood out from the others, It was exactly the same size and exactly the same design as the other houses but the grass in the front and back gardens had clearly not been cut for years and one of the windows on the front of the house was boarded up with three wooden planks. Outside the front door was a broken wooden post box with the name "Cooper" painted on the front of it. The garden had no flowers only dead plants hanging over the pathway and fence which was falling to pieces. Typically this street was a retirement street for the elderly who kept their gardens looking perfect all year round with perfect length grass and perfectly presented flower arrangements but in the house with the boarded window lived a young family who were, to say the least, different from the rest. The man of the house was Tim Cooper; he was a tall thin man with shaved black hair and a permanent five o'clock shadow. He had dark, narrow eyes and little teeth which looked a bit like corn and even had a similar colour. He was a shady, untrustworthy man who was always watching everybody and everything around him like he was guilty of something and was afraid he was going to get caught. The lady of the house was a little fat woman called Alison Cooper; she was a bit older than Tim and was a bit grey of the hair which was always tied back. She had cat like green eyes and a wide, bulbous nose. Alison was a cruel woman who liked nothing more than causing other people sadness. She was loud and quick to anger. The couple had been together for thirteen years now and had lived in the house with the boarded window for ten. They moved into the house from the one bedroom flat they used to live in when Alison became pregnant with their only child, Billy.

Billy was short for his age of ten and was very thin just like his Dad, his eyes were very blue and his hair was long, black and always messy, he was never told when to bathe or to brush his teeth because his parents just didn't care which meant that his hair was always smelly and greasy and his breath could offend a skunk.

The Cooper family didn't have much money as neither Tim nor Alison worked a single day in their lives but always seemed to have just enough to survive. For the most part they lived on benefits which had a very negative effect on Billy especially at school where he was every bully's favourite victim. The other children would constantly harass Billy and tell him that he and his parents were living off their parent's taxes which had obviously come from the other adults around town who had grown tired of the Cooper's. Tim was well known for doing odd jobs around town for extra cash so he and Alison had many connections but no friends or family to speak of apart from each other and their son. Everybody knew them as the family you should stay away from, being tied in with them could only lead to trouble, late at night you could hear them screaming at the top of their lungs at each other till the early hours of the morning, then a few hours later you could see the timid, slow moving shape that was poor Billy sneaking out the house to school.

On this particular morning Billy left the house as he did every day, put his hood up on his rain coat which dragged along the floor as he walked, locked the door and began his walk to school. The school was the oldest building in the town, it had three floors and it had a huge church like roof. There was an old iron fence surrounding the school grounds and a double gate which opened to the stone staircase leading to the front entrance. The school entrance always reminded Billy of a haunted mansion in an old horror film; he got shivers every time he passed through those gates. As Billy walked towards the stairs he was greeted in the way he was every day by the school bully, Frank, and his three sidekicks Darren, Tom and Johnny. Frank was the biggest and the dumbest kid in school, he was tall, broad and overweight with a short temper and a sick taste for causing pain. Darren and Tom were best friends who knew Frank all their lives since all their Dads knew each other from the local pub. The only reason Frank kept them around was because his Dad told him to look out for them. Johnny was an unusual little boy who was very intelligent but really weird; he was always drawing sick pictures of people being murdered and there was a rumour that he killed his cat to see what its insides looked like. He took a laptop to school with him that had stored videos of animals being killed and other depraved things. Billy thought they kept hanging out with him because they were secretly scared of what he could do if they ever rubbed him the wrong way. Either way, whatever trouble Frank decided to cause, his little sidekicks were more than happy to help out in any way they could. On this particular day Frank decided to cause as much pain to Billy as he could and saw his opportunity to do this as the Iron Gate was swinging open. He slammed the gate in Billy's face while the three other boys laughed maniacally as blood poured from Billy's mouth and nose. As the tears in Billy's eyes dripped from his face and mixed with the blood on the tarmac, he looked up to see the four boys walking away in their usual formation. Frank led the way as Darren, Tom and Johnny walked behind him next to each other obediently waiting for their orders. This was a normal thing for Billy, every day he got hurt and tormented by the bullies who loved nothing more than to watch him suffer, but it wasn't just them, all the kids saw him as being a lower form of life that they had a right to torture, even a teacher by the name of Mrs Balterby took pleasure in making Billy's life a living hell.

 Mrs Balterby was a shrill old witch of a woman with long, wavy white hair and a sick sense of humour. She would pick on Billy relentlessly making him look like a fool in front of the other students, nothing went his way and he was starting to tire of his hellish existence.

After he had washed all the blood from his face, Billy went to his classroom. Mrs Balterby was written on the door in thick black letters. Billy slowly walked to the back of the room to take his regular seat slightly further away from the other children when the witch like teacher spotted him and decided to greet him, "oh hello, have a good weekend did you?" she said sarcastically giggling slightly as she spoke "That's it Billy you go sit in the back on your own again. Are you trying to bring more attention to yourself? Try washing your hair for once that would get the whole class turning around in amazement." Billy ignored her but found it very difficult to ignore the piercing laughter of the other children. He sat down and bowed his head so nobody could see his face as he felt it burn as it grew redder and redder but Mrs Balterby wasn't done embarrassing him yet, "Look at me boy. If you don't want to be here you can go, none of us want you here you're a disgrace to this school, this is your last chance. Someone as stupid as you should never be here in the first place, if you don't pass the test your spending a week in detention." Billy looked up at her, "I'll try my best…"

"You'll try your best?" Mrs Balterby looked at him with disgust and the class burst out in laughter. Billy's head sank further towards his desk and the wicked teacher continued her torment, "You said that last time Billy. Here's last week's test, if this is your best you must be mentally ill, nobody can claim this is trying their best." She pointed at Billy's test from the week before which was blank apart from a note that said "I don't understand sorry but don't" and that was it.

Mrs Balterby shook her head at Billy then shouted for the rest of the class to be quite as she began teaching. When the bell rang for the children to go for their first break, everyone headed straight for the playground but Billy waited until everyone was outside so he could find somewhere to be alone until it was time to return to class. He ended up in the boys toilets in one of the stalls where he was certain no one would find him but he should have known better. He heard the entrance door slam open and heavy footprints walk in then the grainy voice of Frank spoke, "come on Billy we've looked everywhere else we know you're here. If you come out we'll go easy on you." Billy knew better than to believe Frank but he heard the doors of the other stalls being opened and knew it was only a matter of seconds before they found him. He saw the bully's feet moving outside the stall he was hiding in and braced himself for what was coming and just as Billy was about to make a plead for mercy as a last pathetic attempt to save himself a bit of pain, the bell rang for them to return to class. The feet disappeared from outside the stall and out of the door to the dark hallway. "Saved by the bell." Billy chuckled to himself as he too returned to his class. The day continued the same way as it did every day with pain and torment for Billy until the final bell rang and Billy was hit with a feeling of relief that for the next twenty minutes he would have peace as he walked home but he knew that once he got there the torment would start up again.

His life was endless pain in his mind. At home he was neglected and made to be afraid of his parents because of their constant fighting, at school he was tortured physically and mentally to the point where he felt like giving up.

When Billy was about to walk on to his street he heard someone calling his name, "Hey!" Billy looked around to see who it was but saw no one. "Hey, freak." Billy didn't have to look around this time, that low grainy voice that spoke with a slow sense of stupidity, he knew it was Frank on his way home to his nice house and nice parents who spoilt him rotten. He tried to run home but tripped over his rain coat that his Dad made him wear because it saved him having to buy a new one. If he wasn't wearing the coat he would have made it home in time but as Billy fell to the floor Frank saw his opportunity and sprinted to him. He kicked the defenceless Billy in the ribs, laughed and walked away chanting the words that were always spoken when anyone saw Billy walking towards them "Billy the freak there he goes, what he is no one knows."

Billy picked himself up from the floor and wiped the tears from his muddy face. His face grew redder again but this time it wasn't embarrassment that brought the blood to his cheeks, it was anger. He picked up the nearest object which happened to be a large stone and threw it with all his strength screaming as he did so. The stone reached the top of the tree's that decorated the street and hit something with a great thud. Something fell to the ground by Billy's feet. It was a bird nest. At this moment something strange happened to Billy, he felt a feeling he had never felt before. When he saw he had destroyed the nest and smashed an egg that was in it he felt powerful. For once he felt like he had control and he smiled to himself as he saw the undeveloped baby bird peeking from within the broken egg lifeless and still. He killed it before it took its first breath and that made Billy feel better than he ever had before, but his anger at Frank still dwelled inside him.

Billy went home feeling more angry than he ever had before because of Frank that day and felt he just couldn't deal with his negligent parents pretending he didn't exist. He walked through the front door and slammed it behind him to let them know he was home. They were arguing when he got there but after the banging of the front door they fell silent. Billy waited for some kind of communication from them. Anything would have been fine in Billy's opinion he just wanted to be noticed by them for once in his miserable life. After a few moments silence they started arguing again and Billy's hopes of finally being acknowledged went up in a puff of smoke. He expected no more from them really, he knew they only had him to get more benefits but this time he felt no sadness, no pain, just more anger. He went up to his room where he felt he belonged, locked the door and started writing on a notebook. He had no thought as to what he was writing; he just let his feelings spill out on the paper like his blood had been spilling on the playground for years now under the force of Frank and his loyal lap dogs Tom, Darren and Johnny. At first it was just gibberish that he wrote but after a while words appeared before him, words like "revenge" and "pain", "kill" and "die". He wasn't afraid by this; anger took his mind far away from his deep sadness. As he wrote the words he got more and more angry, he could feel his blood boiling as the feelings started to take over him until finally he lost it and screamed with all his energy. It was like he was releasing all the pain from his body. He passed out as the air escaped his lungs and didn't wake till the next day.

Chapter two: Heather.

It was a bright sunny morning; the sky was blue and clear of any clouds. Billy woke up to the sound of his parents arguing again, they did this every day at the same time over what Alison was making for breakfast but Billy never had a chance to get what he wanted. He was expected to get himself something whenever he was hungry but was told to leave whenever he was anywhere near his Mum and Dad. The only time food was ever made for him was when Alison made a proper meal for dinner which was very rare and even then he wasn't allowed to eat until she and Tim had finished and left scraps for Billy to salvage for himself.

Billy went downstairs to see if there was any chance of a decent breakfast this morning. As he descended the stairs the voices of his parents became louder and louder, the sound always gave him goose bumps. Billy looked into the kitchen from behind the door so he wouldn't be noticed and saw only crusts of toast on the table. Once again Billy would be going to school on an empty stomach.

As he walked the twenty minute walk to school, Billy noticed some commotion outside one of the houses on his street. The house was owned by a little old woman called Heather Dawson; she lived alone and was well known as a recluse. Her only human contact was when she had her shopping delivered to her house and even then she never said a word, she just took the bag and gave the man some money which was always the perfect amount so she wouldn't have to stay outside for too long. Heather was a small, petite old woman. She was very old and very frail with thin, shoulder length grey hair and grey eyes. Heather's skin was pale and wrinkled and she stood slightly hunched over. Many stories were told about her but most of them were just childish stories that the kids made up to entertain each other. They said things like she was a witch who spent all day making potions and poisons to trick children into coming in so she could eat them or that she was a vampire who would die if she was out in the sun for too long and hunted for people to feed on when the sun came down.

The commotion outside Heather's house was caused by Frank and the rest of the bullies who were throwing rocks at her house while shouting at her to come outside and try to stop them. Billy could see Heather looking at them from behind her upstairs curtains. Billy felt sorry for her, he knew what it was like to fall victim to Frank and his goons and he wished he could do something to help her but fear stopped him from making a move. He looked on as she was getting tormented the way he was every day of his life but did nothing to stop it. He went to school feeling ashamed. Billy was just about to enter the school gates when he suddenly had a strong feeling that he should go back to talk to Heather, he felt that if anyone would understand him it would be her. He looked around to see if any teachers had seen him yet then turned around and started to run as fast as he could away from the many people who treated him as someone who didn't matter. This was the first time he ever skipped school, he was scared that he'd get caught but the thought that he wouldn't have to deal with all the people who made his life hell for a day made him feel excited.

As he approached the house and saw the beautiful statue near the window that was engraved with the words "Heather, you will always be in my Heart" Billy realised that he'd never been this close to it before. The only reason he knew Heather was from hearing people make fun of her at school. Other than the stories the children made up, people said she was an old recluse who couldn't stand the sight or sound of other people. They said she locked herself away because she hated the world and everything in it and it was said that she was given the statue by her fiancé who left her for another woman which drove her insane many years ago.

Billy had to know the truth about Heather, maybe she was just scared of the world because of how she was treated by everyone in it. Billy knocked on the door. The house looked perfect from outside because a young man called Adam came over once a fortnight to do the gardening for her, everyone thought he must be her Grandson but she never came out to speak to him, he just did the gardening and went on his way. After waiting almost ten minutes for Heather to answer the door, Billy decided to try and open it himself. He slowly pulled down the door handle. It was unlocked. As Billy pushed the door open as quietly as he could a smell reached his nostrils, it was like stale bread. The first room he went into was the living room, it was the same size as the one in Billy's house but the furniture was unlike anything he'd seen. The room was covered in old statues and paintings that had all seen much better days. There were two red armchairs and a matching three seat sofa which were covered in dust and cobwebs as were the many bookshelves and ornaments. Billy saw that Heather wasn't in this room so he walked into the kitchen. It was dusty and covered in cobwebs just like the living room and there were loaves of bread half eaten on the counter tops which explained the smell. After seeing Heather wasn't in this room either he began to climb the staircase and as he got to the top he saw that the upstairs was different from the upstairs at his house. His had the bathroom door at the top of the stairs then three bedrooms all quite close together but at the top of Heather's stairs there was just a long narrow hallway with a door halfway along it then one more at the very end. Billy tiptoed down the hallway and slowly opened the first door. It was the bathroom which was covered in grime and lime scale and countless long grey hairs clogging the drains but no Heather. Billy now knew that she must be in the room at the end of the hallway which must be her bedroom. Billy suddenly felt a lot of regret by what he was doing but he was there now and found it too hard to turn and walk away.

Because he knew Heather was in this room for sure he thought it best to knock. This time she answered. Billy heard some movement coming from the room then slow footsteps edging closer to the door. The door opened and there she stood in a long, wight gown.

"Who are you? Why are you here?" she shrieked. Billy froze and though he tried his best could not force a single word from his mouth.

"Answer me or get out. Hurry up!"

Billy was frozen completely still with fear as the old woman stared down at him with those eerie grey eyes but despite his fear he managed to mumble a sentence,

"I know what it's like to be like you please let me explain." But Heather didn't want him to explain, she just wanted him out and let out a scream as she dragged Billy down the stairs; she pushed him out the front door then locked it and screamed one more thing "why can't you all leave me alone."

At that moment Billy realized that Heather thought he was like Frank just trying to cause as much trouble as possible. She didn't know that he just wanted someone to talk to and maybe show him some affection. The anger in Billy started to bubble up again, he knew he couldn't go back to school now without a reason he wasn't there on time and if he went home his parents would show no mercy and he would have hell to pay for skipping school. He decided to take a walk to try and get rid of some of the anger that was so intense now he was physically shaking. He walked down a street he hadn't been on for a long time and saw one of the houses had new people moving into it. There was a dog tied up outside while the new owners were moving everything into the house. The dog kept barking and barking and Billy felt himself get even angrier, he walked towards the dog saying calmly "shut up, please shut up" but the dog kept barking and Billy's head was pounding. It all got too much for him to take and he saw that one of the planks of wood from the fence was loose. Billy ripped the loose plank of wood away from the fence, turned to look at the barking dog and once again asked it to stop barking while he held the piece of wood by his side. The dog kept barking at him and Billy couldn't take it anymore. Billy lifted the wood and began beating the dog around the head with it while he shook violently with all the anger inside him. The dog gave out a yelp then fell silent. Billy knew the dog was dead and with that his anger disappeared. He ran away from the scene of the crime and hid for a while in the woods about a mile from his house. As he sat and thought about what he'd done to the bird nest and that dog, Billy didn't feel worthless for once. The fact that he could have that kind of control over another creatures life made him feel more powerful than he could ever imagine, he ended one life and put a stop to another before it had even began.

After waiting in the woods all day alone with just his thoughts to keep him company, Billy was ready to make his way home when he saw that it was the time he would usually finish school but when he got there it was the same as it always was. After feeling so invincible earlier that day he was suddenly brought back to his twisted reality with his parents fighting none stop and him having to scavenge for scraps of food to eat. He no longer felt powerful but the week would go quickly and he was going to take full advantage of the weekend for once in his life. He needed to feel the way he did earlier more than anything and he would stop at nothing to feel that power again.

Billy went on with the school week the same way as he always did but this time he wasn't letting anything get to him, he was just going through the motions as he anxiously waited for the weekend. Finally after a four more days of being picked on the final bell on Friday rang and Billy ran home avoiding anything or anyone who could slow him down.

Billy slept well that night and dreamt of what had happened during at the start of the week but in his dreams it wasn't just a smashed egg and a dead dog, he dreamt of killing all kinds of animals. He dreamt of how he could make them suffer and call out in agony but to Billy this wasn't a nightmare, this was a fantasy. He woke up with a wicked half smile on his face and he was looking forward to what the day might bring and he wouldn't have to worry about anyone stopping him from doing what he wanted to do because he always had the woods to hide in. that's where he started the day. He got dressed and sneaked out of the house before his parents woke up and went to the woods. When he got there he ducked down under a branch behind some bushes just as he had the day he killed the dog and he just waited for anything to pass him. At first he just saw insects that were killed with no effort with a stamp of his foot or a hit from a stick but eventually a bird landed on the branch above his head. Billy knew as soon as he moved the bird would fly away so he just watched and waited. The bird went further away from Billy so he stayed where he was until there was some distance between them then started stalking it like a lion stalking its prey. The bird finally led Billy to its nest which had no eggs in it this time but it did have three baby birds. Billy started to feel something from his stomach, he was getting butterflies as he grew excited because he knew what he wanted to do, he wanted to murder those birds and he wanted to watch their lives fade away under the force of his hands. He scared away the mother with a simple sudden movement then began to climb the tree. The branch that the nest was on was only a short climb from the ground so he got there quickly and took the nest with the three baby birds back behind the bushes beneath the branch where he liked to hide. Billy began by pulling at their wings and legs making them call out in pain which only egged him on to cause more, then he started to pluck the few feathers that decorated them from their bony bodies. As he went on, Billy got more and more violent with his experiment then half an hour later the birds were dead.

He took his time to torture them separately then finished them off together by dropping a rock on them. He got the rush he was aiming for and relaxed for the rest of the morning beneath the tree right next to the pool of blood and the crushed bodies of the baby birds.

Chapter three: home away from home.

Billy spent a lot of his days searching for animals to take his anger out on now and he kept getting more adventurous with his killings. He would find new interesting ways for quick kills and kills that were long and painful but it was all just a way to distract him from his miserable life.

One day when he grew tired of doing the same thing over and over again, skipping school and killing defenceless animals, Billy decided he should try to speak with Heather again. It had been at least a month now since the last awkward meeting occurred and he decided that no matter what happened it would be unlikely that it would end in the same way so he gathered some courage and set off to her house. When he got there it was exactly how he remembered it, quiet and cold with a strong sense of loneliness. He took a few deep breaths before giving three strong knocks on the door which had seen a lot of punishment from children tormenting and playing pranks on Heather. There was paint and dried egg all over the place that had never been cleaned not even by the young man who did the gardening.

Billy was waiting for a while before he realised that Heather wasn't going to answer the door and decided to sit on the wall beside the house. He didn't want to give in, he wanted to tell Heather everything and he truly believed she would understand him. Billy looked up at her bedroom window and saw that it was open slightly which made him think that she must be in there so he picked up the nearest stone and lightly threw it at the window. Nothing happened so he picked up a few stones and threw them at the window together in a cluster. There was a lot of noise and this time it was followed by the voice of old Miss Dawson screaming as she ran down the stairs to the front door. She opened it quickly saw it was Billy and said "you again? Why can't you all leave me alone why do you insist on making an old woman's life difficult?" Billy was insulted that she put him in the same place as Frank but more than anything he wanted to know her so he spoke with courage, "I'm not trying to make your life difficult I just want to talk." She stared at him waiting for an explanation. He paused for a moment to figure out what he was going to say then as all the courage he had built up fade and a single tear rolled down his cheek he began his plea, "all my life I've been below everyone else, at home I'm ignored, at school I'm tortured daily by the other kids. Even my teachers hate me and I haven't done anything wrong to them. No matter what I do or say I'm never accepted. I know you've felt what I've felt, please, can we talk about it?"

For the first time in a very long while Heather Dawson, the evil old witch of Wesley Road, felt sorry for someone other than herself and spoke back to Billy in a calm, unexpected way, "those boys that vandalise my house. They pick on you don't they?" Billy nodded and waited for heather to continue, "You know what it's like then? Maybe you're different. Okay, come on then." She stepped aside and invited him inside. The house was just as he remembered it with all the cobwebs and clutter and that smell of stale bread wafting around the place as Heather led him to the dining room to talk. When they sat down at the old oak table in the middle of the room Billy began to explain all his feelings and everything he had been going through in his ten years of life, all the pain and all the neglect, all the bullying and abuse. He told her absolutely everything that made him so unhappy and she in turn told him all the things that made her so unhappy. They spoke about how alone they felt in the world like there was nobody else like them, but now they had each other and from then on Billy went to Heather's house every day after school and only ever went home to sleep. One day when Billy was making his way to Heathers house he felt like someone was following him but couldn't see anyone around him.

As he got closer to her house he heard footsteps behind him gradually getting faster and closer and as Billy turned once more to see who was following him, Johnny could be seen diving behind a car. Because Billy knew all of the rumours about him he just walked onward towards Heather's house as if nothing had happened but just as he made the left turn to the street where she lived, Johnny caught up with Billy and grabbed his shoulder.

"Billy stop I want to have a word with you." Johnny said with a strangely genuine tone to his voice. Billy decided he should hear what he has to say since he was away from Frank.

"What do you want?" said Billy and then Johnny released his grip and began to explain,

"I saw you in the woods Billy. I saw what you did to them animals."

"Yeah so what? Everyone knows all the horrible things you've done so what's the difference?"

"There is no difference! That's what I'm saying. Listen, I know we give you a hard time but to be honest I don't like doing it and I don't like Frank, he's just someone to hang out with. Everyone else avoids me because of how I am but Frank likes it, he uses it against everyone but I'm sick of being used. If I start hanging out with you instead of Frank no one will pick on you anymore." Billy knew this was true but could he really trust one of the boys that had laughed at him and made fun of him for so long? Even though it was a risk he figured it was worth taking. "Fine I believe you, I think. How are you going to tell Frank and the others?"

"I'm not going to tell them. Let's just see what happens when they see us together, at school when I'm on my own, come over to me and we'll just stay with each other all day and see what happens."

"Okay I'll do that but I don't think it's going to go well."

Billy saw Johnny at school the next day and they began their plan as Frank turned from Johnny to talk to Darren and Tom. Johnny slipped away from them unnoticed and sat next to Billy on an old worn out bench in the playground. Frank turned to talk to Johnny to realise he wasn't there and as he searched the playground for his missing lap dog he saw him sitting with his enemy. As anger burned from inside Frank a scream escaped his lungs followed by a punch at poor Darren who was just in the wrong place at the wrong time. "What's wrong?" shouted Tom as he saw his friend drop to the floor clutching his stomach, "why did you do that?"

"Look at Johnny with that freak! What's he doing?"

"Their laughing, it's like they're getting along with each other."

"Fine, okay, I don't care if their friends now or whatever we don't need him lads were not going to bother with him, okay?" Tom agreed immediately and after he had picked himself up from the floor where he was crumpled up in pain, so did Darren.

On the days that followed, Frank, Darren and Tom completely ignored Johnny and Billy and just like Johnny had said, Billy didn't get picked on anymore. Things started to look up for Billy from then but his home life was still as bad as it had always been and he lived for the end of the day when he went over to Heathers house where he felt accepted. Johnny was never invited there but on the weekends, he and Billy would head up to the woods to continue their sick pass time of executing animals in new exciting ways. One day when he had just finished school, Billy said Bye to Johnny and made his way to Heathers house for dinner but when he arrived he knew something was different. The house was disturbed like something had just happened there, the grass and flowers were trampled and the gravel that covered the walkway was scattered everywhere. Billy knocked on the door but heard no reply so he opened it and searched the house for Heather. He found her in her bedroom where she usually was but as she looked up to greet him, Billy saw her bloodshot eyes and tears rolling down her cheeks. This was the first time he had ever seen her like this and he felt her pain. She wiped her tears away and began telling him what happened, "it was that fat boy and his friends again, they destroyed my garden. My poor nephew spends so much time on that garden and they've completely destroyed it. Why do they do it Billy? Why can't they leave me alone?" without saying a word Billy turned around and walked out of the house, he was going to make them pay for this somehow, he was going to show them that they can't just do whatever they want all the time. As Billy was walking he thought about what to do but he needed Johnny if it was going to go the way he wanted. He headed to the woods where he knew Johnny would be experimenting with animals just as he always was and began searching for him; he was beneath the big branch where Billy first discovered his sick passion for torture. He told him all about what happened and they both decided something needed to be done.

Chapter four: revenge.

Billy had a lot of problems in his life but he felt that he could take it for as long as it would last, when he saw his friend go through it though it set something off inside him. Usually Billy was mild mannered and took everything with a pinch of salt like it was nothing new, he was used to it all anyway and now he found a way to release his anger by taking it out on animals he felt like things would be fine, but when he saw the tears rolling down Heather's face he knew it had all gone way too far. His new friendship with the former bully Johnny would prove very useful to him in the following days as he knew exactly where Frank, Tom and Darren would be at all times but they still needed a plan to get them back. What could they do to put an end to their cruel actions for good?

One Saturday Billy and Johnny met each other in the woods to talk about how to get revenge, but childish plans of justice soon turned into something a lot more sinister. At first Billy suggested that they find a way to humiliate the boys in public the way that they had humiliated him for so long but Johnny reminded him that they had took it to a new level now that they involved Heather in their cruel pranks so they needed to take it up a notch. They thought of ways they could hurt them emotionally and physically with traps and stunts but still it didn't seem enough. They spent hours thinking of ways to get there revenge but to Johnny there was only one answer. They would always go back to bullying everyone eventually no matter what was done to them unless they were permanently removed from the situation. Johnny wanted them dead. Billy's face went pale as the words "they need to die" escaped Johnny's mouth but he couldn't think of a reason not to do it, it seemed like the only way to him.

They decided that Johnny would arrange to meet them at one of their old hang out spots to try and sort out why they weren't friends anymore while Billy hid ready to kill the bully's and finally bring a bit of peace to the town. In Billy's eyes he would be seen as a hero. When he got home he searched his house for anything he could use to kill the bully's, he searched all over the house but needed to look no further when he opened one of the drawers in the kitchen to reveal a large cleaver with a wooden handle. It stood out from the other knives as the rest were modern with plastic handles and though they were newer and in better shape, he felt drawn to the old cleaver. Billy hid the cleaver under his mattress in his room then went back to the woods to meet Johnny. As Billy was heading down the road he couldn't help feeling scared and anxious about what he and Johnny were going to do. He knew it was wrong to kill people and they weren't like animals that no one would notice, but was it wrong to kill bad people? That question kept playing in his mind but he wanted this more than anything. Finally the torment at school would end for everyone and Billy would be the one to thank.

When Billy got to the woods he found Johnny waiting in the usual place, under the branch. He seemed disturbed by something so Billy rushed over and asked him what was wrong. "Johnny what's wrong? Were still going forward with the plan aren't we?" Johnny looked up and smiled as he gave his reply, "yeah don't worry were still doing it. Did you find anything?"

"Yeah I got this knife from my kitchen drawer."

"That's perfect Billy well done but I just spoke to Frank." Billy thought it was all too good to be true and now he thought it was all going to unravel. "What's happened Johnny? What did he say?"

"Chill out he's just away for the weekend so we'll have to do it next weekend instead." Billy was relieved that there murderous plan of revenge was still on and went home looking forward to the days that would follow. That night he couldn't sleep at all, he felt far too excited by what he and Johnny were about to do. When morning finally came Billy didn't feel how tired he was

because the excitement overpowered all of his senses.
It was a dark, foggy morning which seemed very fitting
to Billy; it set the mood for the dark deed that was soon
to come. He got dressed and quietly l3eft the house as
he did every morning before school then started the day
off with that twenty minute walk to the school gates.
When he got there he could see Johnny on the other
side of the playground talking to Frank, Tom and Darren
and he came to the conclusion that he must have been
making the arrangements for later on.

After speaking with Johnny later that day the plan was
in motion, Frank and his goons were to meet Johnny
inside a tool shed at a house that was for sale on Franks
street. This is where all the Bully's would hang out on
the weekend to talk and play pool as the shed was
converted into a sort of game room by Darren and his
older brother for the boys to stay out of trouble. They
had no idea that today they were going to be in the
worse trouble of their lives. The hours went on and Billy
was growing anxious, he had been trying to stay out of
the way of everyone all day while Johnny was
pretending to be on their side again. Finally that final
bell that signalled the end of school rang and Billy
jumped to his feet and sprinted out of the building to
the place he was to hide until Johnny had the Bully's in
the shed. Billy waited and waited feeling the adrenaline

flowing through his body as he clutched his knife ready to end Heathers torment until he heard the voices outside the shed. Butterflies were fluttering in his stomach creating a strange mixture of fear, anger and excitement. They walked in led by Johnny followed by Frank then Tom and Darren but something was wrong. Tom and Darren were carrying something into the shed with them. Billy poked his head out from his hiding place slightly to try and get a better look but when he did he realised that he had been betrayed. He had been made a fool of because as the boys walked into the light Billy saw that the thing they were carrying was that old statue of Heathers which she loved dearly. It was all a prank. Johnny must have been setting him up all along without anyone knowing not even Frank. Now it was perfectly clear though and as Frank picked up a sledge hammer and brought it down on the statue with all his might, Billy lost all feeling and acted without thinking even for a slight moment what he was doing. He leapt from his hiding place letting out a roar as he plunged the knife into the back of Johnny. The Bully's screamed with terror and fled the scene as Billy smiled down at his lifeless victim pouring out blood onto the shed floor. It was a new chapter for Billy and no one was going to stop him from getting his revenge.

Chapter 5: Barely Human.

After feeling the flash of adrenaline and emotional release of killing another human being, Billy was numb to his surroundings. All he knew is that something changed in him when he felt that cleaver tear through Johnny's flesh and come to a sudden stop as it hit bone. He no longer felt fear or loneliness but he didn't know how long it would last. Maybe this escape from reality was only temporary as the adrenaline pumped through his veins and when it was over he would be brought back to his pitiful existence. He wasn't ready for that yet, not while those three pathetic bullies were still out there somewhere.no, it wasn't going to end this way. In Billy's mind it wouldn't be justified until they were all dead. In his warped opinion, death was the only suitable punishment.

While searching the town for his next victims, Billy grew angrier and angrier as his mind played through all the horrible things they had done to him and everyone else over the years. His cleaver was concealed under his coat tucked into his trousers and he could feel the blood growing cold as it trickled down his leg. As he stopped to wipe the blood away with the bottom of his t-shirt he heard some noises from a tree across the road from him. He looked up to see what was making the noise and as his eyes reached the very top of the tree, Tom and Darren were jumping from it into a bush in a nearby garden. Once again the adrenaline took over Billy's actions and he set off chasing the boys. Darren was always a good runner so he had no problem navigating through the gardens at top speed but Tom was not so fortunate. He stumbled as he tried to jump over a fence to the next garden and rolled over in agony as his ankle twisted backwards under the force of his own weight. He tried to pull himself up on a swing set but as he got up to his knees, Billy was already too close and kicked him in his deformed ankle. Tom screamed in pain as he crumbled to the floor to which Billy let out a loud hearty laugh before saying the last words Tom would ever hear, "Look what you've done! You've made me like this and now you're going to die!" he laughed again as he brought the knife down to Tom's eye level and thrust it upwards into his face "two down. Two to go." He climbed to the top of the swing set to see if he could see where the other boys were but saw nothing.

Everything that had happened to Billy up to this point in his life had twisted and warped his personality and seeing how evil people could be when the bully's destroyed Heather's statue took away the last piece of his humanity. Now all he was just a creature living by instinct and the only thing he needed to do was erase the lives of the bully's. He didn't want to eat he didn't want to sleep or drink or play like a child should. All he wanted was to see the faces of the boys who caused him all this pain as they died in a pool of blood.

Billy searched the town for hours until he ended up at a closed down shop at the edge of a street he wasn't familiar with. He noticed that the door was hanging open slightly and that maybe one of the boys was in there. As he climbed through the gap he thought to himself that it was far too small for big fat Frank to get through but maybe little Darren had thought it the perfect place for him to hide. He looked around quietly at everything in the shop. There wasn't much in there apart from a few empty bookshelves which made him remember that it used to be a bookshop that his Mum used to drop him off at for a couple of hours every Saturday evening while she was off doing something she never spoke about. He remembered it well now and as the thoughts of him feeling scared and lonely came back to him, a burst of rage caused him to throw all the bookcases down one by one. As the last bookcase was thrown across the shop, Darren leapt to his feet. "Billy please it wasn't my idea I didn't even want to do it I swear." Darren kept trying to explain how he had nothing to do with it but it wasn't all about the statue anymore, it was out of Billy's control now. As Darren made a last attempt to escape by throwing an old till through the window and jumping out of it Billy raised the cleaver and threw it with all his strength. As Darren was running down the street he fell to the floor as the blood soaked knife caught him in the back of his head and ended his short life instantly. Satisfied with what he had done, Billy slowly walked past Darren's lifeless body with a smile on his face as he took back his knife and set off to find Frank.

There was just one more left to go now, the worse one, the one that convinced the other kids to pick on Billy so much. Billy was so empty inside now that he was like a machine that's been programmed to do one thing and one thing only and it was impossible for him to resist his murderous temptations. He was no longer a little timid boy who got bullied at school; he had no remorse or feelings towards what he was doing. All that was left was anger and the need for revenge, he didn't even think about what would happen to him when it was all over. As Billy set off through the woods to Frank's house he heard screams and then sirens drawing closer towards him but he paid no attention as he made his way to his final victim. As he got to the house Billy saw that the car was parked outside it which meant Franks parents were in there with him. He looked up to Frank's bedroom window and saw that the light was on. Maybe he could sneak in and finish his task without the adults noticing. He began to climb the drain pipe to the left of franks window. As he got closer he could hear the TV in his room getting louder. He was definitely in there, it was now time to end all this. He climbed through the open window as quietly as he could and looked around the room but saw no one there. "He must be here" he whispered to himself. He saw a wardrobe at the opposite end of the room and the space under the bed; these were the only hiding places available. He looked under the bed but only saw a few old teddies' under there, "I know you're in there Franky" he sang. "Time to end this." He opened the door and there he was huddled in the wardrobe terrified of what was going to happen. Frank screamed for his parents who darted up the stairs to aid their only child and crashed through the door just in time to see their son push Billy down. Frank got away and his mum followed him to see what was wrong but Billy wasn't ready to give up, he looked up at Frank's dad then dropped to the floor to conceal the cleaver. "Are you all right? Little boy are you a friend of Frank's? what's happened?" he walked towards Billy to check if he was okay but at that Billy took the cleaver and chopped at the man's leg bringing him down to Billy's level, then with one clean blow to the throat, the man bled out on the floor and died in his son's bedroom.

Billy had to get to Frank now and as he walked to the top of the stairs he saw him with his mother frozen with terror as she tried to comfort him. This was it, this was the end. Billy ran down two steps at a time and finished the woman off easily with a sweep to the back of her head then pounced at Frank bringing him to the floor. "Time to pay Frank. Time to die." He slowly slit Frank's throat so he could see the pain in his eyes and the screams from his mouth. It was done. No more bully's, so what next?

Billy walked out of the front door with the bloody knife still clutched in his tiny hand. He saw the flashing lights of the police cars as they screeched to a halt on the front lawn. The sirens were deafening, the lights blinding. Screams pierced through the evening air like a hot knife through butter and as a police officer exited one of the cars and called out for Billy to drop to the floor, something clicked. Billy froze and let out a shriek of rage then set off running to the police officer with his bloody weapon held out in front of him to put an end to the officer's life. A gun shot echoed through the air as Billy raced to the officer. A sharp pain through his stunned Billy and brought him to the floor. He looked up at the officer to see that it was Heather's nephew, the one who did her gardening. He then looked around to see where the shot had come from. He gazed back towards the house as his eyesight began to fade. At the end of the garden by the gate stood Heather holding the weapon that brought him down. Billy's eyes closed as he drew his last breath. His pain was fading and it was his only true friend that brought him peace. Or so he thought.

Chapter six: life after death.

Billy was very young and wasn't quite sure what he believed about God and The Devil, he had no idea what happened to you when you died. He was told that if you did good things you went to heaven and if you did bad things you went to hell but what if you did something bad for good reasons? What if you sinned against a bad person to bring justice to a good person? Billy was soon to find out that two wrongs certainly don't make a right and that what we do on earth, determines our fates for eternity when we die.

Flames roaring all around him and screams of pain echoing in the distance. Billy opened his eyes as the screaming became louder and closer. He was surrounded by screams and trapped by the flames. Billy stood up to take in his surroundings and after a few minutes pondering what had happened he came to the only explanation. He was dead and this was hell. As he looked around he saw the flames slowly die down and reveal his everything. What he saw made Billy realise what he had to do. But that's another story.